DR. CAT

For Ing Hoffman and Anna Burton,
good mothers, good physicians

PUFFIN BOOKS
Published by the Penguin Group
Penguin Books USA Inc., 375 Hudson Street, New York, New York 10014, U.S.A.
Penguin Books Ltd, 27 Wrights Lane, London W8 5TZ, England
Penguin Books Australia Ltd, Ringwood, Victoria, Australia
Penguin Books Canada Ltd, 10 Alcorn Avenue, Toronto, Ontario, Canada M4V 3B2
Penguin Books (N.Z.) Ltd, 182-190 Wairau Road, Auckland 10, New Zealand

Penguin Books Ltd, Registered Offices: Harmondsworth, Middlesex, England

First published in the United States of America by Viking Penguin,
a division of Penguin Books USA Inc., 1989
Published simultaneously in Puffin Books
Published in a Puffin Easy-to-Read edition, 1995

1 3 5 7 9 10 8 6 4 2

Text copyright © Harriet Ziefert, 1989
Illustrations copyright © Suzy Mandel, 1989
All rights reserved
THE LIBRARY OF CONGRESS HAS CATALOGED THE PUFFIN BOOKS EDITION UNDER
THE CATALOG CARD NUMBER 88-62152.

Puffin Books ISBN 0-14-037467-1
Printed in the United States of America

Puffin® and Easy-to-Read® are registered trademarks of Penguin Books USA Inc.

Printed in the United States of America

Reading Level 1.7

DR. CAT

Harriet Ziefert
Pictures by Suzy Mandel

PUFFIN BOOKS

Ring! Ring!
Ring-a-ling!

Wake up, Dr. Cat!

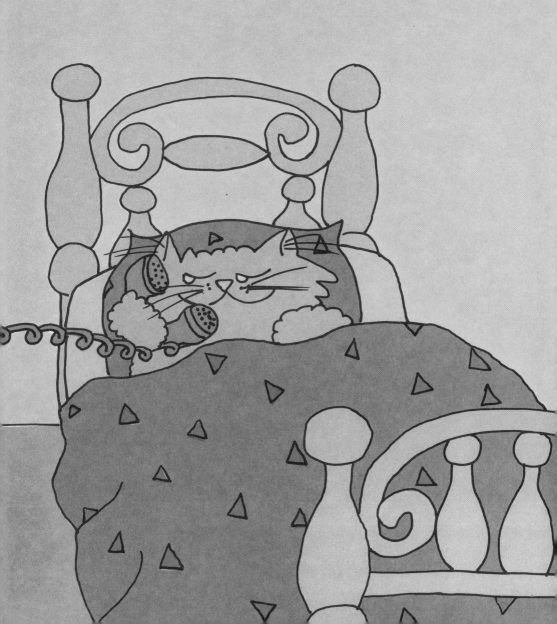

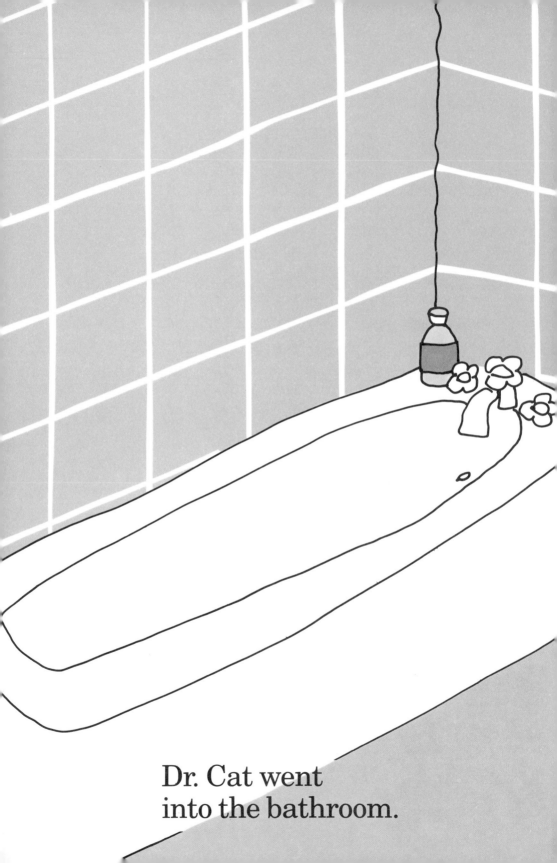

Dr. Cat went
into the bathroom.

He combed his whiskers.

Then he got dressed.

He put on pants...

a shirt...

a tie...

and a white coat.

Dr. Cat put his bag
on his bike.

He rode to his office.

"Good morning, Dr. Cat,"
said Tim, Jim, and Kim.

"Good morning, Dr. Cat,"
said the nurse.

"Who's first today?"
asked Dr. Cat.

"Not me!" said Tim.
"Not me!" said Jim.
"Not me!" said Kim.

"Somebody has to be first,"
said Dr. Cat.

"Tim and Jim will be first,"
said their mother.

"I'm going to check your ears," said Dr. Cat. "Who's first?"

"You first!" said Tim to Jim.
"You first!" said Jim to Tim.

"I'll be first," said Dr. Cat.

So Tim checked Dr. Cat's right ear.
And Jim checked his left ear.

Then Dr. Cat checked
Tim and Jim.

He checked their ears.
He checked their noses.

"Now I'm going to check throats," said Dr. Cat. "Who's first?"

"You first!" said Tim to Jim.
"You first!" said Jim to Tim.

"I'll be first!" said Dr. Cat.
So Tim and Jim checked Dr. Cat.
"AHH!" said Dr. Cat. "AHH!"

And Dr. Cat checked Tim and Jim.
"Ahhh!" said Tim.

"Ahhhhhh!" said Jim.

"Let me listen first," cried Tim.
"No, me first!" said Jim.

"I'm first," said Dr. Cat.

Dr. Cat listened
to Tim's heart beat.
Ker-thump! Ker-thump!

Then he listened
to Jim's heart beat.
Ker-thump! Ker-thump!

"Give Jim a shot!" said Tim.

"No shots today!" said Dr. Cat.
"But who wants to peek inside
my doctor bag?"

"Me first!" said Tim.
"No, me first!" said Jim.

"They can look together,"
said their mother.

"Good idea!" said Dr. Cat.
"Then you're both first!"